SCIENTIFIC AMERICAN EDUCATIONAL PUBLISHING

GET BUILDING!

10 FUN ENGINEERING PROJECTS

BRING SCIENCE HOME

Published in 2023 by Scientific American Educational Publishing in association with
The Rosen Publishing Group 29 East 21st Street, New York, NY 10010

Contains material from Scientific American, a division of Springer Nature America, Inc., reprinted by permission as well as original material from The Rosen Publishing Group.

First Edition

Editor: Jennifer Lombardo
Designer: Rachel Rising

Activity on page 5 by Science Buddies (February 2, 2012); page 11 Science Buddies/Ben Finio (February 21, 2019); page 16 by Science Buddies/Megan Arnett (March 29, 2018); page 23 by Science Buddies/Ben Finio (November 3, 2016); page 27 Science Buddies/Ben Finio (May 19, 2016); page 34 Science Buddies (July 16, 2015); page 39 Science Buddies (June 11, 2015); page 44 Science Buddies (January 29, 2015); page 50 Science Buddies (May 29, 2014); page 55 Science Buddies (February 27, 2014).

Photo Credits: pp. 3, 4, 5, 8, 9, 13, 16, 20, 25, 26, 27, 31, 34, 36, 37, 39, 41, 42, 44, 47, 48, 50, 52, 53, 55, 59 cve iv/ Shutterstock.com; pp. 4, 5, 11, 16, 23, 27, 34, 39, 44, 50, 55 Anna Frajtova/Shutterstock.com.

Cataloging-in-Publication Data
Names: Scientific American.
Title: Get building!: 10 fun engineering projects / Scientific American.
Description: New York : Scientific American Educational, 2023. | Series: Bring science home| Includes bibliographic information, glossary and index.
Identifiers: ISBN 9781725348912 (pbk) | ISBN 9781725348929 (library bound) | ISBN 9781725348936 (ebook)
Subjects: LCSH: Architecture-- Juvenile literature | Engineering-- Juvenile literature | Physics-- Juvenile literature | Science projects-- Juvenile literature
Classification: LCC TA149 S35 2023 | DDC 620 --dc23

Manufactured in the United States of America

CPSIA Compliance Information: Batch #CWRYA23. For further information contact Rosen Publishing, New York, New York at 1-800-237-9932.

CONTENTS

* THESE ACTIVITIES INCLUDE SCIENCE FAIR PROJECT IDEAS.

INTRODUCTION

Engineering is all around us. We often take it for granted, but without it, we wouldn't have bridges, skyscrapers, tunnels, and a lot of other things! By doing the activities in this book, you'll learn how much science it takes to engineer the things we use every day.

Projects marked with include a section called Science Fair Project ideas. These ideas can help you develop your own original science fair project. Science fair judges tend to reward creative thought and imagination, and it helps if you are really interested in your project. You will also need to follow the scientific method. See page 61 for more information about that.

Earthquake-Proof Engineering for Skyscrapers

IT'S TIME TO SHAKE THINGS UP A LITTLE! LEARN HOW ENGINEERING CAN KEEP TALL BUILDINGS STANDING DURING EARTHQUAKES.

PROJECT TIME

120 to 180 minutes

KEY CONCEPTS

Engineering
Architecture
Physics
Earthquakes

Have you ever wondered how tall skyscrapers can stand up so impressively to the force of gravity? What about more violent forces, such as those produced by earthquakes? A well-planned and tested design, when combined with the right materials, can keep a building intact through all sorts of shakes and quakes.

Once the tallest buildings in the world, the Petronas Towers in Kuala Lumpur, the capital of Malaysia, stand at an amazing 1,483 feet (452 m) tall. Because Malaysia is in an area that experiences frequent earthquake activity, the towers had to be designed to withstand the lateral shaking force that is experienced during a quake. Can you, as an amateur architect and engineer, design a structure that can withstand lateral movements similar to that of an earthquake?

BACKGROUND

Architects and engineers must design buildings to withstand a variety of forces, some stronger than others, from many sources: gravity, people inside, weight of building materials, weather and environmental impacts. If the design is stable, these forces will not weaken the structure or cause it to collapse.

Lateral shaking is the force that can cause the most damage to a building during an earthquake. As you might have guessed from its name, this force usually occurs in a direction parallel to the ground. Designing a building to have lateral resistance is helpful not only for preventing quake damage, but also damage from other lateral forces, such as wind. Engineers can test how well a building will hold up to lateral force by placing a model of it on a "shake table," which moves horizontally to replicate the stresses created by an earthquake.

MATERIALS

- LEGO bricks
- Large, flat LEGO baseplate
- Metric ruler
- Three-ring binder (an old one that is okay to take apart)
- Scissors
- Four small rubber balls (each the same size, about 1 inch, or 2.5 cm, in diameter)
- Two rubber bands (each about 3 inches, or 8 cm, or longer when flattened and doubled on itself)

PREPARATION

- Carefully cut the front and back covers off of the three-ring binder with scissors. (This might be a good task for an adult.)
- Place the two binder covers on top of one another and secure them together by stretching a rubber band around each end, about 1 inch (2.5 cm) from the edge of the boards.

- Insert the rubber balls between the boards at each corner, placing them about 2 inches (5 cm) in from the edges.
- Attach a large, flat LEGO plate to the top by slipping the plate underneath the rubber bands. Your "shake table" is now ready to shake some towers!

PROCEDURE

- Practice creating a lateral shaking movement with the shake table by pulling its top layer horizontally out of alignment and then letting it go.
- Gently try pulling the top layer as far out of alignment as you feel comfortable with (and without damaging the shake table), then measure the distance of displacement, which is the horizontal distance between the top and bottom layers.
- Build four or more LEGO towers of increasing height on a nearby surface. Use the same base size and shape for each tower, so that the size of the towers' footprints is the same and only their heights vary. *What are the heights of the different towers?*
- One at a time, starting with the shortest tower and progressing to the taller ones, secure each LEGO tower in the center of the shake table's top surface. To test each structure, create a lateral shaking movement using the same distance of displacement you previously measured. *Did all, none or some of the towers fall? If some fell and others did not, what were the differences in height between these towers? In general, did the taller towers fall more frequently than the shorter ones?*
- **Tip:** If none of the towers fell, try testing this activity with taller towers and/or a smaller base size. If all of the towers fell, try testing this activity with shorter towers, a larger base that takes up more space, and/or a smaller distance of shake-table displacement.

SCIENCE FAIR IDEA

In this activity, you kept the footprint of each tower the same and only changed the height. Try testing LEGO towers with different-size bases. *Do you think that by changing the footprint, you could make taller buildings more stable?* You could also calculate the area of the base (by multiplying its length times its width in centimeters) and divide this by the height for each tower to get the ratio of base to height. *How do the towers' base-to-height ratios compare with how they perform on your shake table?*

SCIENCE FAIR IDEA

Try building towers out of a different material that allows you to test different structural designs. Good materials are straws, popsicle sticks, or toothpicks and marshmallows. Try comparing square designs to triangular or hexagonal designs. Try adding extra structural elements to your designs. *Can you design a stabler tower? How tall can you build it before it loses stability?*

OBSERVATIONS AND RESULTS

In general, did the taller towers fall whereas the shorter towers remained standing? If you varied the footprint of the towers, were the ones with larger footprints generally more stable than the ones with smaller footprints?

Structures that are tall or skinny are generally less stable, making them more likely to fall when exposed to lateral forces, whereas ones that are shorter or wider (at the base) are generally more steadfast. Architects and engineers use all kinds of innovative techniques along with these basic principles to build amazing skyscrapers. Building heights keep creeping upward as technology allows engineers to safely build higher.

One major technological breakthrough that allowed for the creation of skyscrapers in the late 1800s was the development of a material that was lighter and stronger than previously used materials: steel. Before this, buildings were mostly made of brick and stone. Architects and engineers designed skyscrapers with a steel framework that supported the building's weight, which meant that the walls no longer had to be load-bearing (as they had previously been). This development, along with other innovative ideas and materials, allowed for the creation of skyscrapers—and as our technologies continue to improve, we will be able to reach ever closer to the sky.

CLEANUP

Put away the materials you used. Throw out the remains of the binder.

How Tall Can You Build a Tower Before It Topples?

CAN YOU MAKE A TOWERING TOWER THAT DOESN'T TIP OVER? USE PHYSICS TO ENGINEER YOUR WAY TO BUILD TO NEW HEIGHTS!

If you've ever built towers with blocks, you've probably knocked some of them over—either on purpose or by accident. Sometimes your tower gets too tall and wobbly, and you just can't keep it standing! In this activity, you'll learn about the trade-offs you need to make when building a tower that is tall *and* stable.

PROJECT TIME

45 to 60 minutes

KEY CONCEPTS

Physics
Engineering
Ratio
Stability
Forces

BACKGROUND

What determines if a block tower will stay standing or fall over? Think about a single rectangular block placed horizontally on the ground. The block has a wide base relative to its height, so it is very stable. If you push on its side with your finger, it will probably slide sideways but not tip over. Now take the same block and stand it vertically on one end. The base is now narrower relative to its height. If you push on the block near the top, it will probably fall over instead of sliding. What if you add more blocks? Two rectangular blocks stacked on top of each other horizontally will be much more stable than if you stack the same two blocks end to end vertically. The tower's stability depends on the ratio of its width to its height. This poses a challenge: Given a limited number of blocks, how can you build a tower that is as tall as possible—but also stable? (That is, it won't tip over easily when you push it or blow on it.) In this project, you will try it and find out!

Note that this same concept applies to real buildings. Very short structures, such as single-story houses, are generally very stable. Tall structures that get narrower as they reach the top, like pyramids, are also very stable. Tall, skinny structures such as skyscrapers can be much more susceptible to natural disasters, including high wind and earthquakes, which can cause them to topple. It takes a lot of extra engineering to make sure they stay safe!

MATERIALS

- Toy cardboard or wooden blocks, or an assortment of empty cardboard boxes—cereal, tissue, shoe boxes, etc. (Do not use plastic snap-together blocks.)
- Pencil and paper
- Chair to stand on or an adult to help you put blocks on the top of your tower (optional)
- Fan (optional)

PREPARATION

- Make sure you have enough open floor space to build a tall tower and that it will not break anything if it falls over.

- Gather all your blocks before you start. Count how many blocks you have and sort them roughly by size (small, medium and large).
- Make sketches of a few different block tower designs. Try to make the towers as tall as possible—but also plan for them to be stable so they won't fall over easily.

PROCEDURE

- Try building one of your tower designs. If the tower gets higher than you can reach, stand on a chair or ask an adult for help to add more blocks. *Can you finish building the tower before it falls over?*
- If you manage to finish building the tower, try gently tapping it with your finger in a few places. *Does the tower fall over?*
- If your tower fell over, think about how you can redesign it to be more stable. *Do you need to sacrifice some height to accomplish this?*
- If your tower did not fall over, push the limits! *Can you make it even taller while keeping it stable?*
- Keep iterating (redesigning and rebuilding) your tower until it is stable but you cannot make it any taller without making it unstable.

EXTRA

Aim a fan at your tower to simulate wind. *Does your tower stay standing?*

OBSERVATIONS AND RESULTS

Building the tallest possible tower may at first seem very simple—just stack all of your blocks vertically end to end, one on top of the other. That should give you the maximum possible height, right? Technically, yes, but it will also result in a tower that is extremely unstable because it's too tall and skinny. It might fall over on its own before you're even done building! Conversely, you can build an extremely stable tower by making it very short and wide—but then it won't be very tall! The best solution probably lies somewhere in between, with a tower that is wider at its base than at its top. You probably had to go through multiple iterations of building your tower until you found the design that worked best. This is a normal feature of the engineering design process.

CLEANUP

Put away the materials you used.

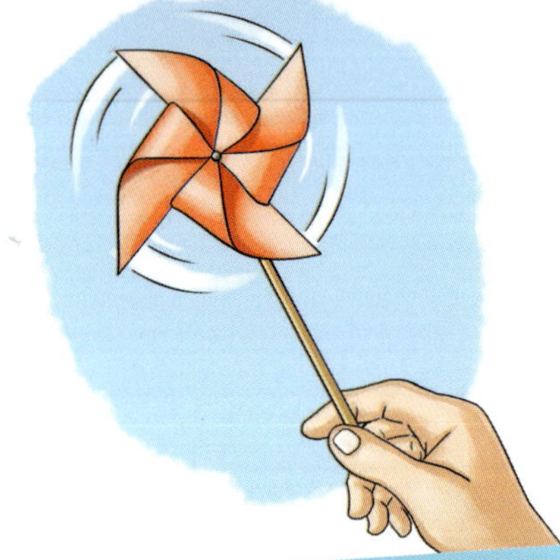

Just Keep Spinning

Find the Best Pinwheel Design!

FIND THE MOST EFFICIENT SPIN—WITH THIS BREEZY ENGINEERING ACTIVITY.

PROJECT TIME

45 to 90 minutes

KEY CONCEPTS

Physics
Engineering
Mechanical energy
Electrical energy
Wind

Wind energy is becoming more and more popular across the U.S.—maybe you've even seen a wind farm close to where you live! In 2015, approximately 7 percent of the electricity used in the U.S. was generated by wind. So when you switch on a lamp in your house, that light might be coming from wind energy!

Wind energy is generated by wind turbines. These machines can look like giant pinwheels, and their job is to turn energy from the wind into mechanical or electrical energy. Believe it or not, the wind turbines we use today are based on designs that are more than 4,000 years old!

In this activity, we'll be exploring different turbine designs by testing pinwheels and learning about the factors that can improve their performance.

BACKGROUND

Wind turbines convert wind into mechanical or electrical energy. One type of wind turbine, the windmill, has been used all over the world for thousands of years to convert wind energy into mechanical energy for tasks such as grinding grain and moving water. More recently, wind farms that use turbines to convert wind into electrical energy have become increasingly popular. In some states, wind is quickly becoming a major source of electricity. In 2015, for example, more than 30 percent of the electricity used in Iowa came from wind!

In general, wind turbines all have the same basic components: blades on a rotor connected to a shaft, both of which are turned by the wind hitting the rotor blades. To make wind energy as efficient as possible, engineers have experimented with many different wind turbine designs. For example, turbines can rotate on a horizontal or vertical axis and have large or small blades. In some cases, they can even be bladeless!

Variations in the design of wind turbines are based on where the turbine will be located and how environmental factors will affect its performance. The goal, however, is always to maximize the amount of energy extracted from the wind. You will explore one of these factors—blade shape—to determine how it affects the efficiency of a pinwheel.

MATERIALS

- Four pieces of 8-by-11-inch (20 by 28 cm) construction paper
- Stickers or tape
- Three flat-ended pins or thumbtacks
- Three thin dowel rods or large craft sticks
- Scissors
- Ruler
- Glue
- Adult helper
- Pen or pencil
- Clock or timer
- Hammer or soft mallet (optional)
- Fan (optional)
- Hair dryer (optional)

PREPARATION

- Cut two 8-by-8-inch (20 by 20 cm) squares of paper from two pieces of construction paper. Place one square on top of the other and line up all the edges, then glue these two pieces together, making one 8-by-8-inch (20 by 20 cm) square. Tip: for a pretty pinwheel, use two different colors of paper.

- Use a third piece of construction paper to cut out eight 4-by-2-inch (10 by 5 cm) strips of paper. For each pair of strips, place one strip on top of another and line up all the edges, then glue those two strips together. When you are finished, you should have four of these 4-by-2-inch (10 by 5 cm) strips.

- Use your last two pieces of construction paper to cut out eight triangles, each with a base of 3 inches (7.5 cm) and height of 4 inches (10 cm). For each pair of triangles, place one triangle on top of the other and line up all the edges, then glue those two triangles together. When you are finished, you should have four triangles, each 4 inches (10 cm) tall with a 3-inch (7.5 cm) base.

PROCEDURE

- This activity requires handling sharp materials. Please ask an adult to help you with these steps!

- Start with your 8-by-8-inch (20 by 20 cm) square of paper. Fold the square in half diagonally and make a crease. Open it up and fold it diagonally again, this time in the opposite direction. Make a crease, then open the paper back out to the square.

- Use your scissors to cut from each corner along the diagonal fold, stopping 1.5 inches (4 cm) from the center.

- You now have a square with four wings or petals. Starting with the topmost petal, gently fold down the right corner of the petal and hold it in the center of the square. Try not to crease the paper. Repeat this with each remaining petal, holding each corner in place in the center with your hand. **Tip:** Ask an adult to help you hold the petals in place as you work your way around the square.
- Once all four petals have one corner folded down to the center, hold them in place with a sticker or tape.
- With the help of an adult, push your thumbtack through the sticker or tape at the center of the pinwheel. Use the tack to attach the pinwheel to the top of a dowel rod. (Use a hammer or soft mallet for this step if necessary.) Make sure the pinwheel is held securely but can still turn on the thumbtack.
- Take your four 4-by-2-inch (10 by 5 cm) strips of construction paper. Fold each strip vertically down the center, then open it back up again so that the paper forms a "V."
- Use your ruler to measure 0.5 inch (1.2 cm) from the short edge of each strip. Use your pen or pencil to make a small mark in the center of the strip, 0.5 inch (1.2 cm) from the end.
- With the help of an adult, stick the thumbtack through the mark on each strip until all four strips are attached to the tack. Spread them out from one another so they point in four different directions. Use the tack to attach this second pinwheel to the top of a dowel rod. (The hammer or soft mallet may be necessary for this step.) Make sure the pinwheel is held securely but can still turn on the tack.
- Finally, fold each of the four triangles you cut out down the center from apex to base, and then open them back up so each piece of paper forms a "V" shape.
- Use your ruler to measure 0.5 inch (1.2 cm) from the apex of the triangle. Mark this point with your pen or pencil.

- With the help of an adult, stick the thumbtack through the mark on each triangle until all four triangles are attached to the tack. Spread them out from one another so they point in four different directions. Use the tack to attach this third pinwheel to the top of a dowel rod. (Use your hammer or soft mallet for this step if necessary.) Make sure the pinwheel is held securely but can still turn on the tack.
- Test each of your pinwheel designs. If it is windy outside, you can do this by taking them outside and holding them in the breeze. Or you can hold them each in front of a small fan, under a ceiling fan, or use a hair dryer on the lowest, cool setting to blow air at your pinwheel.
- For each test, hold your pinwheel to the wind and count the number of full rotations in one minute. Also observe how well the pinwheel performs in the wind. *Which pinwheel seems the sturdiest? Which one seems the weakest?*

EXTRA

Test other pinwheel designs. Observe which factors seem to be the most important for creating the best pinwheel.

OBSERVATIONS AND RESULTS

In this activity, you designed and tested three different model pinwheels. Each design you tested had different-shaped rotor blades. You should have found the first pinwheel, with the folded-over blades, rotated the fastest and most smoothly when placed in front of a fan or in a breeze. The triangle- and rectangle-shaped blades probably did not spin as quickly or as efficiently as the first one you tested.

The difference in performance of each pinwheel was the result of the different-shaped rotor blades that you tested. The first pinwheel's blade design allowed each blade to capture the most air as it rotated. To understand why this made it move faster, imagine a swimmer racing through the water. With each stroke, a good swimmer will keep their hand closed and slightly cupped to try to capture the most water. This allows the swimmer to "push" against more water and propel themselves forward. You can imagine if they spread their fingers wide and allowed the water to flow through, they wouldn't be able to push themselves through the water as quickly.

Your first pinwheel design is based on the same principles. Because it's folded over, it acts like a pocket for collecting air. The more air it can collect, the more efficiently it will be pushed around the rod. The other two pinwheel designs did not collect air in the same way. The wind moved past but did not bump into the blades on those versions; therefore, they weren't pushed as quickly or smoothly as those on the first design.

Now that you know the basics of pinwheel rotor blade design, try to make the most efficient pinwheel you can!

CLEANUP

Put away the materials you used. Throw out or recycle any scraps, and wipe down your work area.

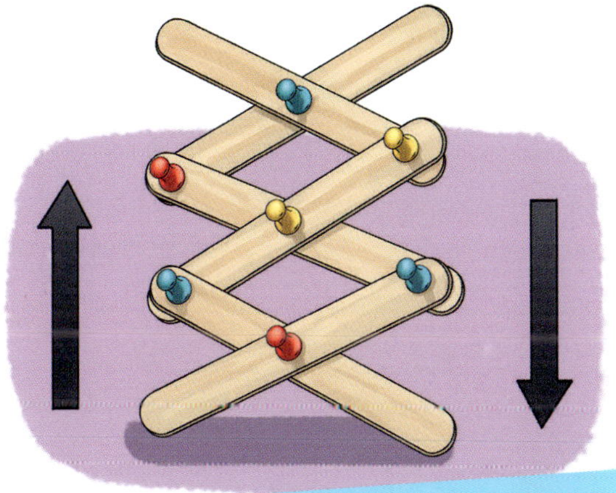

Build a Cardboard Scissor Lift

RAISE YOUR KNOWLEDGE TO NEW HEIGHTS—WITH PHYSICS!

Have you ever wanted to reach something way up high on a shelf? Or have you ever watched construction workers who need to reach up a tall utility pole? A scissor lift is a device that can extend to a great length but also fold up very compactly. In this project, you will build your own scissor lift from common household materials!

PROJECT TIME

30 to 60 minutes

KEY CONCEPTS

Physics
Mechanics
Linkages
Geometry

BACKGROUND

Mechanical linkages are a type of machine generally made up of rigid bars connected to each other by rotating or sliding joints. When combined, links and joints can be used to create many complicated motions that are used in machines all around you. They can be used to convert motion from one type to another. For example, a linkage in a car engine converts the back-and-forth motion of the piston to rotational motion, which is eventually transferred to turn the car's wheels. Linkages can be used to amplify both force, such as in a pair of pliers, and motion. An example of the latter is a lever in which one side is twice as long as the other. When you push down on the short end, the long end will move twice as far. (Note that in both cases energy is conserved—you can never get "free" work out of a linkage.)

In this project, you will build a mechanism called a scissor lift. Such lifts are used in construction equipment to elevate workers to high places. More generally, they are a type of pantograph. A scissor lift uses an accordion-like motion to contract and stretch out, allowing it to both fold compactly and extend much beyond its original length. Try this project to build your own—and see what heights you can reach!

MATERIALS

- Corrugated cardboard
- Pushpins or thumbtacks
- Modeling clay or Play-Doh
- Scissors (and an adult to help cut and use pushpins, if necessary)
- Ruler (optional)

PREPARATION

- Cut the corrugated cardboard into at least six equal-size strips. The exact dimensions do not matter, but roughly 0.7 to 1 inch (2 to 3 cm) wide and 4 to 6 inches (10 to 15 cm) long is a good start.

PROCEDURE

- Carefully use pushpins to poke through the center of two strips and join them to form an "X."
- Form an X with a pushpin and each remaining pair of cardboard strips.
- Now, use pushpins to join the top of one X to the bottom of another X, as shown in the illustration on p. 23. It is important that the pushpins be in about the same location on each strip. (For example, don't put one right in the middle and another one close to the edge.)
- Continue joining the top of one X to the bottom of the next X with pushpins. Make sure you alternate left to right which piece of cardboard is on top and which is on the bottom—this will keep your mechanism flat.
- Use small bits of modeling clay or Play-Doh to cover the points of the pushpins sticking through the back of the cardboard.
- Now, lay your entire scissor lift flat on a table. Gently hold the free ends of one X with your fingers. Try lightly pulling them away from each other. *What happens?*
- Now try gently pushing them toward each other. *What happens?*

EXTRA

Use a ruler to measure the total length of your scissor lift when it is contracted all the way and when it is extended all the way. *How much can it change its length?*

EXTRA

Cut more cardboard strips and extend your scissor lift. *How long can you make it?*

EXTRA

Your cardboard scissor lift is a nice example of how the mechanism works, but it is not very sturdy. *Can you build a sturdier scissor lift out of different materials? Can you put a "claw" on the end so you can use it to reach and grab for things?*

OBSERVATIONS AND RESULTS

You should find that when you pull the ends of an X apart, your scissor lift contracts (all the Xs get shorter and squished). When you push the ends of an X together, the scissor lift extends (all the Xs get tall and skinny). Depending on exactly how you cut your pieces of cardboard and where you put the pushpins, it should be able to extend to roughly twice its original length.

Because your scissor lift is made out of cardboard, there should be some flexibility in the joints, and your pin placement does not have to be perfect. If you were not careful enough about how you cut the cardboard or where you put the pins, however, your scissor lift might jam, or be unable to move. To work properly, the links must form parallelograms in between each pair of X's—four-sided shapes whose opposite sides are the same length and always parallel to each other. If you cut pieces of cardboard to different lengths or do not put the pins in the exact same spots on each link, then the links might not form parallelograms when you connect them, and your scissor lift will not work.

The modeling clay mainly serves to protect you from pricking your fingers with the pushpins but does not do a very good job holding the scissor lift together. To build a sturdier scissor lift, try using something like wooden craft sticks instead of cardboard, and have an adult use pliers to bend the ends of the pushpins at 90-degree angles to prevent them from falling out of the holes.

CLEANUP

Put away the materials you used. Throw out or recycle any scraps. If you want to keep your scissor lift, put it in a safe place where it won't get squashed by anything heavy.

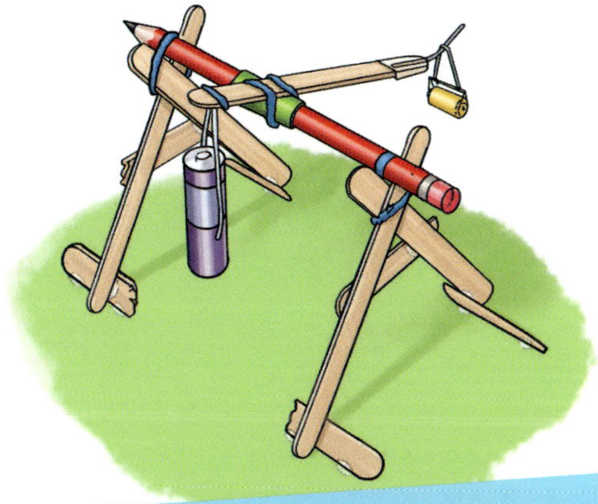

Build a Mini Trebuchet

BUILD YOUR OWN MINIATURE MEDIEVAL LAUNCHER—AND SEE HOW PHYSICS AND ENGINEERING CAN HELP YOU GET THE BEST DISTANCE!

PROJECT TIME

60 to 90 minutes

You probably know what a catapult is. In the Middle Ages, armies would use them to hurl stones at castle walls. However, did you know about an even bigger type of medieval siege weapon called a trebuchet? Try this project to build a miniature version!

KEY CONCEPTS

Physics
Engineering
Potential energy
Kinetic energy
Conservation of energy

BACKGROUND

A catapult works by storing elastic potential energy—the type of energy you get from stretching something such as a rubber band or a spring—and rapidly converting it to kinetic energy (the energy of motion) of a projectile (in this case, a cotton ball).

A trebuchet works differently. It relies on gravitational potential energy—the type of energy you get by raising something up off the ground. A trebuchet has a lever arm with a large, heavy counterweight on one end and a smaller projectile on the other end. When the counterweight is raised up, it has lots of gravitational potential energy. Then the counterweight is allowed to fall, rotating the lever arm and converting that potential into kinetic energy in the projectile, which is flung through the air.

Many medieval trebuchets were larger and could hurl projectiles even farther than catapults. Get ready to build your own!

MATERIALS

- Piece of corrugated cardboard, about 1 foot by 1 foot (30.5 cm by 30.5 cm)
- Popsicle sticks
- Scissors
- Pencil
- Jumbo or "milkshake" straw
- Glue (A hot glue gun is best if available, but use caution and adult assistance when using hot glue.)
- Tape
- Rubber bands
- String
- Paper clip
- AA battery

PREPARATION

- Assemble all your materials in a location that is open and clear of people, animals, or breakable objects so that you can test your trebuchet. **Safety note:** Never aim projectiles at people or animals. A toy trebuchet might seem harmless, but even a small projectile can cause eye damage.

- To build your trebuchet, you will build a frame that looks almost like a swing set. It will have two "A-frame" shaped pieces on the sides and one crossbar on the top. There is more than one way to do this, so the procedure described here is just one method. For example, you could decide to build the entire frame out of pencils instead of popsicle sticks, and you can choose whether you want to use tape, glue, or rubber bands to secure the different joints. Think of this as an engineering design project—there is no single "right answer" or correct way to build the trebuchet. You can modify your design based on your own ideas and the materials you have available.

- Start out by building the two side A-frame pieces. Take five popsicle sticks and cut one of them in half. Use two long pieces and one half-piece to form an "A," but make sure you cross the long pieces slightly at the top to form a miniature "V" shape. This will leave a small notch for the pencil to rest in later. Glue them together and repeat with the other pieces.

- Carefully cut slots in your piece of corrugated cardboard that will allow your A-frame pieces to stand up straight, a few inches apart from each other. Stick the ends of the A-frame pieces into the slots. Reinforce the connections with glue or tape and some extra popsicle stick pieces if necessary so they remain standing on their own.

- Now you will build the trebuchet's arm. Carefully cut two small notches on either side of a popsicle stick close to one end. The notches should be wide enough to slide in a piece of string. This will help hold your counterweight in place.

- Attach a small loop of string to your AA battery using tape or rubber bands. Hang the battery from the notches in the popsicle stick. If necessary, make the notches deeper or secure the string with tape, glue, or rubber bands. *Why do you think it is important in this design to have a counterweight? How does it help employ the idea of gravitational potential energy?*

- Unbend one end of a paper clip so it is almost, but not quite, straight. Attach the remaining flat part of the paper clip to the other end of the popsicle stick, with the straightened part pointing outward and up (away from the counterweight). This will serve as a hook to hold the "sling," which in turn holds the projectile.

- Remove the eraser from the pencil and attach it to a small loop of string. Hang the eraser from the paper clip hook.

- Cut a small section of milkshake straw, about 1 inch (2.5 cm) long. Attach this perpendicularly to the popsicle stick arm using glue, rubber bands, or tape. The straw should be much closer to the counterweight than it is to the hook. (This distance is something you can try adjusting later.)

- Slide the pencil into the milkshake straw.

- Place the pencil into the two V notches on top of your A-frame pieces. Secure it in place with rubber bands. This forms a crossbar and completes your trebuchet's frame. The straw and pencil form a pivot and should allow the arm to rotate. (We do not recommend using glue for this step—that way you can remove the crossbar and swap out the arm to make changes.)

- Make sure your trebuchet is sturdy and the frame holds together. Try rotating the arm with your hand. If any of the joints seem weak or the frame wobbles significantly, reinforce them with tape, glue, or rubber bands.

PROCEDURE

- Now it is time to test your trebuchet. Use one hand to pull down on the eraser. This should raise the counterweight up in the air. Then, making sure no people, animals, or breakable objects are nearby, let go. *What happens when you let the eraser go? Does it get launched forward? Does it go straight up in the air? Does it fail to release at all?*

- Now you might need to tinker with your trebuchet in order to get the best launch. Try pulling the eraser under the trebuchet frame. It is okay if the eraser is resting on the ground and there is slack in the sling. When the counterweight falls, it will drag the eraser along the ground and then pull it up into the air. *Can you find the best starting point for the eraser? What makes it go the farthest?*

SCIENCE FAIR IDEA

There are lots of variables you can tinker with to improve your trebuchet's performance. Try changing any of the following things to see how they affect the distance the eraser is thrown. *Can you optimize your design to toss the eraser as far as possible?*

- The size of the counterweight: Try using lighter (or heavier) batteries. *What impact do you think the weight of the counterweight will have on your projectile?*
- The length of the lever arm: Both the overall length and the ratio between the distance from the pivot to the counterweight and the pivot to the sling. *What happens if you move the pivot so it is exactly in the middle of the arm? What if you glue multiple popsicle sticks together to make a longer arm?*
- The length of the sling: *What happens if you make it longer or shorter?*
- The shape of the hook: *What happens if you bend the paper clip so it is straighter or more curved or if it is cut to be shorter?*
- The weight of the projectile: *What happens if you use something other than an eraser, such as a small balled up piece of paper?*

OBSERVATIONS AND RESULTS

When you pull down on the eraser, this causes the battery to lift up in the air, giving it (gravitational) potential energy. When you release the eraser, the battery falls and its potential energy is converted to kinetic energy. As the arm swings, the sling holding the eraser slides off the hook and the eraser's kinetic energy causes it to fly through the air as a projectile.

Depending on exactly how you built your trebuchet, the results you see will vary. Remember that there is no single "correct" way to build the trebuchet. A well-built trebuchet should be able to hurl an eraser a few feet. Don't get discouraged if at first your trebuchet launches the eraser straight up in the air or fails to release it at all. You should be able to tinker with your design a bit (see the Science Fair Idea) to get your eraser to launch.

CLEANUP

Put away the materials you used. Throw out or recycle any scraps. If you want to keep your trebuchet, put it in a safe place. If not, dismantle it and put back or throw out the items you used to make it.

Popsicle Stick Trusses
What Shape Is Strongest?

WHAT MAKES A STRUCTURE SUPERSTRONG? WOULD YOU BELIEVE IT CAN COME DOWN TO SIMPLE SHAPES? LEARN HOW WITH THIS FUN ENGINEERING ACTIVITY!

Have you ever driven across a bridge or seen a building that is under construction and noticed the large metal support girders? What about wooden beams in a house that is under construction? Did you notice how sometimes the supports form different geometric shapes, such as triangles or squares? In this project, you will be a structural engineer and make your own "support" shapes out of popsicle sticks. What shape do you think will be the strongest?

PROJECT TIME

30 to 60 minutes

KEY CONCEPTS

Physics
Geometry
Engineering
Trusses

BACKGROUND

When civil engineers build large structures such as bridges and buildings, they have to take into account how forces—such as gravity, compression, tension, and torque—will act on the building materials. Gravity is constantly working to pull materials—especially heavy ones—toward Earth. The weight of cars driving across a bridge, for example, can push (creating compression) or pull (tension) on a structure, causing them to break if they are not designed properly. Engineers also have to design structures to handle torque, or twisting. An example of torque is when you turn a screwdriver to twist a screw or if you were to hold a ruler in both hands and try to bend it.

Bridges and buildings usually have their frames built as a "truss," or a series of beams that are connected at their ends. The engineer's goal is to design a truss that will slightly flex, but not bend or break—even with strong forces acting on it. In this project, you will make trusses by connecting popsicle sticks end to end with binder clips. Can you guess what simple geometric shape will resist bending the most? Get ready to find out!

MATERIALS

- Popsicle sticks (at least seven)
- Small binder clips (at least seven)

PROCEDURE

- Clip two popsicle sticks together end to end using a binder clip.
- Hold one end of each popsicle stick in each hand. Gently try to twist them back and forth, rotating around the joint where they are connected by the binder clip. (Do this by sliding the flat surfaces of the popsicle sticks against one another; do not try to break them by bending them.) *How easy is it to rotate the popsicle sticks around the joint?*
- Now make a square out of popsicle sticks that are connected by binder clips at the four corners.

- Grip two adjacent popsicle sticks with your fingers and gently try to rotate them relative to the joint that connects them. *How easy is it to rotate the popsicle sticks? What happens to the shape of the entire square?*
- Grip two popsicle sticks that are opposite one another and gently try to slide them back and forth parallel to one another. *How easy is it to slide the popsicle sticks back and forth? What happens to the shape of the entire square?*
- Now make a triangle out of popsicle sticks that are connected by binder clips at the three corners.
- Grip two adjacent popsicle sticks with your fingers and try to rotate them just like you did with the square. *What happens? Can you rotate the popsicle sticks or does the triangle maintain its shape? How does it compare with the square?*

EXTRA

If you have more popsicle sticks and binder clips, try making a larger truss structure out of multiple connected squares and/or triangles. *What happens when you push, pull, or twist different parts of the truss? Does one shape (triangle or square) tend to hold its shape better, whereas the other one slides around?*

EXTRA

Try adding a diagonal across the square, dividing it into two triangles. (Secure two popsicle sticks together with multiple binder clips to make a single, longer stick that cannot rotate). *Can you still easily rotate the square?*

EXTRA

If you have building toys available, such as K'nex, Tinkertoys, or LEGO Technic pieces, try using them to make trusses of different geometric shapes. (Note that this will not work with regular LEGO bricks; you need beams with holes that can be connected by pegs.) *Do you get the same results as you did with popsicle sticks?*

OBSERVATIONS AND RESULTS

You should have found that it was very easy to rotate the popsicle sticks in your square truss. When you rotate two adjacent popsicle sticks, or slide two sticks that are opposite one another, they all stay connected, but the entire square deforms to form a parallelogram—which might be fine for a popsicle stick structure, but disastrous for a building!

When you try to rotate the popsicle sticks in the triangle-shaped truss, however, they do not move. The triangle design is stronger—the popsicle sticks are arranged in such a way in this shape that when you push or pull on them, none of them can rotate.

This happens because of something engineers call "degrees of freedom." The square truss has one degree of freedom, which means it can move in one direction (in this case, a rotational direction—it can rotate from a square to a parallelogram). The only way to prevent the square from rotating at all is to pinch down very, very hard at the joints (imagine using much stronger binder clips). You can now see why it would not be good to only use squares when building structures—all of the joints would have to be superstrong! The triangle, however, has zero degrees of freedom—all of its popsicle sticks are fixed in place and cannot rotate. This means you can build a truss structure out of triangles that does not rotate or deform—even though the joints are only lightly held together by binder clips.

CLEANUP

Put away the materials you used.

Paper Bridges

WHAT SHAPE MAKES THE BEST BRIDGE? BECOME A PAPER BRIDGE ENGINEER AND LEARN ABOUT HOW SHAPE PLAYS A ROLE IN DESIGNING STURDY STRUCTURES. CAN YOU COME UP WITH AN EVEN STRONGER SHAPE?

PROJECT TIME

60 to 75 minutes

KEY CONCEPTS

Physics
Gravity
Weight
Civil engineering

Have you ever walked, ridden your bike, or driven in a car over a long bridge? Bridges have to be sturdy enough to support the weight of many people and cars without collapsing. One important part of designing a bridge is selecting the right materials. Another is making sure those materials comprising it are shaped in a way that makes them as strong as possible. In this project, you will build a simple "bridge" using materials you already have on hand—paper and tape! Can you build a miniature bridge that doesn't collapse?

BACKGROUND

If you take a piece of paper and try to bend or flex it, it will bend very easily. How hard it is to bend a material is referred to as the material's bending stiffness. A stiffer material will be harder to bend. However, if you roll the paper tightly into a tube or fold it into an accordion shape, it becomes much harder to bend. Why does this happen? It is still the same material, but its shape also affects how easily it bends.

Both the bending stiffness and the shape are very important for civil engineers to consider when designing bridges. Lots of cars drive over a bridge all at once, and cars are very heavy. If the bridge's bending stiffness is not high enough, it could sag under the weight of all the cars or even collapse! So, whether a bridge is made out of stone, wood, steel, or another sturdy material, civil engineers still have to carefully consider its shape.

MATERIALS

- Four thick books (such as school textbooks, cookbooks, etc.) that are roughly the same thickness
- At least six pieces of construction paper
- Scotch tape
- Ruler or measuring tape

PREPARATION

- Create two stacks of two textbooks each. Place them just under 2 feet (0.6 m) apart from each other on a table, floor or other flat surface.
- Line up two pieces of paper end to end, so the short edges are overlapping just slightly (by about a quarter of an inch, or 0.6 cm). Use long strips of Scotch tape to bind the pieces of paper together on both sides. These two pieces of paper will make one "bridge."

- Repeat this process for four more pairs of paper, so you can make five bridges total.

PROCEDURE

- Take one of your taped-together bridges and lay an end on top of each pile of textbooks, with about half an inch (1.2 cm) of overlap. You might need to slide your textbooks closer together or farther apart a bit. *What happens to the paper? Does it stay up in the air or sag down under its own weight?*

- Now take your next taped-together bridge. Tightly roll it into a long tube and use a few pieces of tape to hold the tube shut. Place the tube on top of your textbooks as you did before. *What happens to the tube? Does it stay up or collapse?*

- Take your next taped-together bridge and fold it into a "W" shape lengthwise (meaning, when you look at the short end, you should see a W shape). Do this by folding in half lengthwise first, then folding each half again in the opposite direction (for a total of three fold lines, dividing the paper into four equal sections). Place the W shape on your textbooks like you did before. *What happens this time?*

- *Which bridge stayed up best? Which one collapsed fastest?*

SCIENCE FAIR IDEA

Create two new bridges and come up with your own designs. *What other shapes can you think of?* Now test them out. *How well did they fare compared with the first three bridges?*

SCIENCE FAIR IDEA

Put your bridges higher up—for example, between two tables and chairs. Use some string and a plastic cup to hang weights from them. (You can use coins as weights.) *Do certain shapes hold more weight than others?*

OBSERVATIONS AND RESULTS

You should have found that the flat pieces of paper bent very easily and sagged down under their own weight. Bending or rolling the pieces of paper, however, increases their bending stiffness quite a bit, allowing them to form a bridge between the stacks of textbooks. Try to look around you for examples of this principle in everyday life. For example, you might have desks and chairs at school with metal legs. Are the legs flat pieces of metal or are they tubes? Why do you think cylindrical tubes might be better for supporting the weight of a person than flat pieces?

CLEANUP

Put away the books, tape, and ruler. Throw out or properly recycle your bridges.

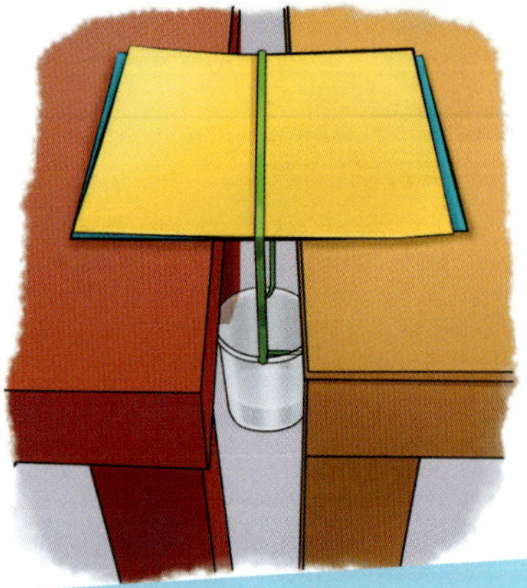

Superstrong Science

Explore Nanotechnology Using Paper

LEARN HOW STRENGTH AND SHAPE ARE RELATED IN THIS SUPERPOWERED ACTIVITY.

PROJECT TIME

60 to 75 minutes

KEY CONCEPTS

Nanotechnology
Matter
Strength
Engineering

Have you ever seen a superhero movie where the superhero relies on a superstrong material, such as Wolverine's adamantium claws, Captain America's vibranium shield, or Iron Man's suit of armor? While scientists and engineers in comic books work on creating fictional materials to help superheroes win the day, real-world scientists and engineers are actually already creating superstrong materials that could have a variety of uses—from improved bulletproof vests to stronger ropes to lighter bikes to better spaceships. In this activity, you'll explore how simply the shape of molecules in a material can dramatically affect its strength, using nothing more than sheets of paper. Who knows—maybe this will set you on the path to designing your own superpowered objects!

BACKGROUND

Nanotechnology is the science of studying materials at the "nano" scale, or the scale of individual atoms and molecules. Just how small is the nanoscale? A nanometer is one billionth of a meter. A typical human hair is about 100,000 nanometers wide—so a nanometer is really small!

The structure of a material at the nanoscale can dramatically change how it behaves. For example, pencils contain graphite, which is made up of carbon atoms that are arranged in sheets and can easily slide around. It's easy to write with a pencil because the graphite sheets easily rub off onto paper. Carbon atoms, however, also make up some of the world's strongest materials—diamonds! In diamonds, carbon atoms are tightly packed together, making them so hard that they can cut steel.

Scientists are working on another superstrong version of carbon atoms called carbon nanotubes, which consist of sheets of carbon atoms rolled into tiny cylinders! Although this makes individual carbon nanotubes incredibly strong, mass-producing carbon nanotubes remains a challenge. In this activity, you'll compare the strength of paper that is stacked in sheets versus rolled in tubes to simulate the difference between flaky graphite and carbon nanotubes.

MATERIALS

- Two tables, chairs, or desks of equal height
- 12 pieces of paper
- Scotch tape or rubber bands
- Plastic cup
- Sturdy string or thin ribbon
- Hole punch or sharp knife (Please use adult supervision when using the knife.)
- Many coins, all of the same type (for example, about 250 pennies or about 100 quarters)

PREPARATION

- Set up your two identical tables, chairs, or desks so they are next to one another, with a 2- to 3-inch (5 to 7.5 cm) gap in between.
- Roll six of your pieces of paper into tubes about 1 inch (2.5 cm) in diameter. Use Scotch tape or rubber bands to hold the paper in tube shapes.
- Use the hole punch or knife to punch two holes on opposite sides of the cup, near the rim at the top. Cut a piece of string several feet long and tie one end of the string securely to each hole.

PROCEDURE

- Stack six sheets of paper on top of one another so they bridge the gap between your two tables. Center the sheets across the middle of the gap.
- Hang the plastic cup from the sheets of paper so the string goes directly across the middle of the sheets (centered in the gap between the tables), and tie the two ends of the string in a knot to secure it. *Do the papers sag at all under the weight of the plastic cup alone?*
- One by one, add pennies to the plastic cup until the paper falls. (Note: If the string breaks before the paper, retie the knot or use a thicker string, then restart the activity.) *How many coins does it take to make the paper fall? What happens to the paper? Does it bend gradually or does it fold sharply in the middle?*
- Now, lay your six tubes of paper next to one another, with each one crossing the gap between the tables. Center the tubes across the middle of the gap. Make sure the tubes are pressed up against one another with no space in between.

- Hang the plastic cup from the tubes so the string goes around all six tubes and is centered in the gap between the tables. Tie the string ends in a knot. *Do the tubes sag at all under the weight of the plastic cup alone?*

- One by one, add your coins to the plastic cup until the tubes fall. (Note: If the string breaks before the paper, retie the knot or use a thicker string, then restart the activity.) *How many coins does it take to make the tubes fall? What happens to the tubes? Do they bend gradually? Do they fold sharply in the middle?*

- *Which structure could hold more coins, the flat sheets of paper or the paper tubes? How do you think this relates to what you read about graphite and carbon nanotubes in the Background section?*

EXTRA

Repeat this activity, but tape the flat sheets of paper together at the edges so they cannot slide with respect to one another. You can also try taping the paper tubes together. *How does this change your results? Do the structures get stronger or weaker when they are taped together?*

SCIENCE FAIR IDEA

Repeat the activity with different diameter paper tubes—for example, diameters of 0.5 inch and 2 inches (1.2 cm and 5 cm). *As the tubes get bigger (or smaller), can they hold more or less weight?*

SCIENCE FAIR IDEA

Repeat the activity with other folded or rolled structures that you invent. *For example, what happens if you fold a sheet of paper into a rectangular tube instead of a cylindrical one? How does the strength of the tubes change as you vary their shapes? Which shape is the strongest?*

OBSERVATIONS AND RESULTS

Were the rolled sheets of paper stronger than the stacked sheets of paper?

You should have found that sheets of paper rolled into tubes were much stronger, and therefore could hold the weight of more coins, than sheets of paper that were simply stacked on top of one another. Just like the sheets of carbon atoms in the graphite of a pencil, stacked sheets of paper are "flaky"—they can easily slide around on top of one another, which makes them very weak and unable to hold a lot of weight. When a sheet of paper is rolled into a tube, it becomes much stronger, even though it is still the same sheet of paper. This is similar to how carbon atoms become much stronger when they form tiny cylinders in carbon nanotubes. Note that in this activity, you modeled the differences between graphite sheets versus carbon nanotubes by comparing paper sheets versus paper tubes. Although physics behaves differently at the nanoscale of individual atoms compared with the "macroscale" (or the scale of everyday objects that we are used to), the general principle is still the same—you can drastically change the strength of a material simply by changing its shape.

CLEANUP

Put away the materials you used. Throw out or recycle any scraps.

Sphere-Based Science

Build Your Own Geodesic Dome

HOW STRONG IS A DOME? FIND OUT IN THIS TASTY ENGINEERING ACTIVITY.

Have you ever seen a geodesic dome? Geodesic domes are spherelike structures made up of interconnected triangles. A famous geodesic dome is Walt Disney World's Spaceship Earth at Epcot, but geodesic domes are also commonly found as climbing domes at playgrounds. In this activity, you will get to build a simple geodesic dome using gumdrops and toothpicks. Get ready to do some tasty engineering!

PROJECT TIME

30 to 45 minutes

KEY CONCEPTS

Architecture
Geometric shapes
Engineering
Physics

BACKGROUND

A geodesic dome is a structure made of struts that are connected to one another to approximate the shape of a sphere (or part of a sphere). Richard Buckminster "Bucky" Fuller, an American inventor, architect, author, engineer, designer, and futurist, patented the geodesic dome in the 1940s and made it popular. Spaceship Earth at Epcot is a geodesic dome that is a complete sphere shape, but many other geodesic domes, such as climbing domes at playgrounds and some greenhouses, are often only part of a sphere.

Typically, the struts or ridges of a geodesic dome are joined together in triangles, with the points of the triangles creating the sphere's "surface." The edges of the triangles form big circle-like shapes, or geodesics, over the dome's surface. The struts form a rigid network that transmits stress forces throughout the structure, allowing geodesic domes to support a surprisingly large amount of mass compared with the mass of the structure itself.

MATERIALS

- 11 gumdrops (Alternatively, jelly beans or other semifirm, chewy candies may be used.)
- 25 toothpicks

PREPARATION

- Gather the 11 gumdrops and 25 toothpicks that you will use to make your geodesic dome.

PROCEDURE

- Attach five toothpicks together using the gumdrops to form a flat pentagon (five-pointed) shape. You should have a gumdrop at each point and a toothpick along each edge.
- Poke two more toothpicks into each gumdrop, arranging the new toothpicks so that they are pointing up.

- Take five new gumdrops and attach them to the top of the new toothpicks, putting two toothpicks into each gumdrop, to form triangles. (The pentagon should form the base of the triangle, and the new gumdrops should form the top point.) You should end up with five triangles this way. *Why do you think the geodesic dome is made out of triangular shapes?*

- Attach a toothpick between the top points of the triangles you just made, connecting the triangles together. This uses five toothpicks and will create another pentagon, this time at the top of the dome.

- Take five more toothpicks and poke one into each of the five gumdrops that make up the top pentagon. Arrange the new toothpicks so that they are pointing up. Then poke all five toothpicks into a gumdrop in the middle and at the top of the dome. Your geodesic dome is complete!

- Gently press down on the top of your geodesic dome. If it does not break, try carefully pressing down on it a little more. *How strong is your dome? Are you surprised by how well it can support your hand as you press down on it?*

EXTRA

Try doing this activity again, but this time use long wooden skewers instead of toothpicks. *Is one geodesic dome stronger than the other? If so, which one is stronger and why do you think this might be?*

EXTRA

Try adding some mass on the top of your dome, such as heavy envelopes. *How much mass can your dome support before it fails? Are you surprised by how strong it is? When the dome fails, how does it fail? Can you figure out a way to make it even stronger?*

EXTRA

The geodesic dome you made in this activity uses a relatively simple design. You could try making a more complicated or larger one. *Can you build a much larger geodesic dome? What about one that uses multiple different strut lengths? How does a more complicated design compare with the one used in this activity?*

OBSERVATIONS AND RESULTS

Could your geodesic dome easily support your hand as you pressed it down on the dome, even when you increased the pressure?

A geodesic dome's design allows it to support a surprisingly large amount of mass compared with the structure's mass itself. Because of this, you should have seen that the geodesic dome could easily support your hand as you pressed down on the top of the dome, even when you increased the pressure a little. You would need to apply a lot of pressure before the dome would fail. The struts of a geodesic dome—made here by toothpicks—are arranged to make triangles, which overall create a rigid network that disperses any stress forces applied to the top of the dome through the rest of the structure.

Because the geodesic dome approximates a sphere, it has a relatively low surface-area-to-volume ratio (that is, its volume is relatively large compared with its surface area) and it can enclose a large amount of volume when compared with the mass of the structure itself.

CLEANUP

Throw out the toothpicks and eat the gumdrops!

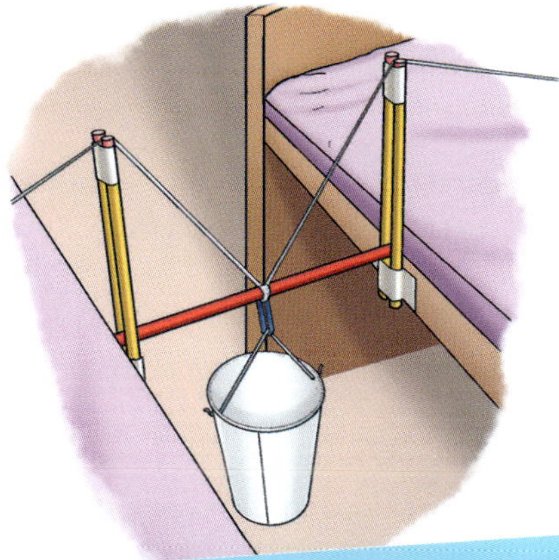

Suspension Science

How Do Bridge Designs Compare?

IN THE BATTLE OF THE BRIDGES, WHICH WILL WIN? USE ENGINEERING TO FIND THE ANSWER!

Have you ever ridden in a car driving across a suspension bridge? Suspension bridges, with their tall towers, long spans, and gracefully curving cables, are beautiful examples of the work of civil engineers. How do the cables and towers withstand the load of the bridge—including you and the car you're in? Can a suspension bridge carry a greater load than a simple beam bridge that doesn't use cables? You can try to answer these questions in this suspenseful science activity!

PROJECT TIME

60 to 90 minutes

KEY CONCEPTS

Bridges
Forces
Load
Engineering

BACKGROUND

A beam bridge is the simplest type of bridge. It is typically supported by a raised part on either end. For example, a beam bridge could be as simple as a wood plank put down to cross a stream.

Suspension bridges are a bit more complicated. They comprise a deck (the long, straight part that includes the road), cables, and towers. The cables stretch between the towers and help support the weight of the deck and its load. In this type of bridge, the cables are under tension and the towers undergo compression.

Suspension bridges might seem complicated, but for spanning long distances, they can also be the most economical—they require less material per foot than a simpler beam bridge does. Because suspension bridges are relatively flexible, however, high winds and other forces can be a serious problem. The dramatic collapse in 1940 of the Tacoma Narrows Bridge in Washington State is an infamous example of this. (You can watch a video of the disaster on YouTube.)

In this activity, you'll build and test two types of bridges: a basic suspension bridge and a beam bridge. Which type of bridge do you think can support a heavier load?

MATERIALS

- Seven disposable plastic drinking straws
- Masking tape or painter's tape
- Thread
- Scissors
- Four paper clips (At least two should be large ones.)
- Paper cup, at least 8 ounces (0.2 L)
- Many coins, all the same type (For example, you should have at least 150 quarters or at least 325 pennies.)
- Two chairs, tables or desks that can be arranged to build a bridge between, and on which tape can be used

PREPARATION

- If your straws are the bendable type, cut the flexible part off so that you are left with a long, straight, nonbendable straw piece. Cut a total of six straws this way. Make sure they are all the same length; trim some if necessary. (If you are using nonflexible straws, use the whole straws for the long pieces.)
- Cut the seventh straw to make two short pieces of straw, each about 1 inch (2.5 cm) long. Make sure they are both the same length. (If it has a bendable part, cut your short pieces from the other end.)
- Tape two of the long straws to each end of one of the short pieces of straw.
- Then, tape the long straws together at their other ends. You should have an elongated triangle shape. This is one of the towers for your suspension bridge.
- Repeat this process with two new long straws and the other short straw piece to build the second tower.
- Tape one tower to the edge of a desk, table, or chair. The short straw piece should be at the bottom of the tower (and the pointy end without a short piece should be at the top). Tape the second tower to a second piece of furniture at the same height. Position the towers far enough apart so that you can fit the remaining straws between them.

PROCEDURE

- Place a long straw between the towers so that its ends rest on the short pieces. This straw is the deck. You now have a simple beam bridge. *Can you see how this is a beam bridge? How do you think it would be different from a suspension bridge?*

- Make a load tester for your bridge by unbending a large paper clip into a V shape. Poke the ends of the paper clip into opposite sides of a paper cup, just below the thick rim at the top.
- Use a second large paper clip to hang the load tester over the bridge deck. Do this by attaching the two large paper clips together, and then sliding the new one around the bridge deck straw. Slide the cup to the middle of the straw deck.
- Add coins (all of the same type) one at a time into the load tester. Keep a count of how many coins you are adding. *How many coins does the cup hold before the bridge fails? How does the bridge fail?*
- Begin turning your structure into a suspension bridge. Pick a new long straw to serve as the deck.
- Cut a piece of thread about 3 feet (0.9 m) long. Tie the center of the piece of thread (which will act as your bridge cable) around the middle of the new bridge deck straw. Place the straw between the towers as before.
- Pass each end of the thread over a tower and down the other side. To anchor the suspension bridge, tie each end of the cable around a paper clip. Slide the paper clips away from the towers until the cable pulls tight. Then tape the paper clips firmly to the furniture.
- Attach the empty load tester cup as you did before. Again, add coins (all of the same type as before) to the cup, one at a time. *How many coins does the cup hold before the bridge fails this time? How does the bridge fail?*
- *Overall, which bridge design is stronger? Is it a little stronger or a lot stronger? Why do you think you got the results that you did?*

EXTRA

Test each bridge design a few more times, using a new bridge deck straw each time. *Are your results always the same?*

EXTRA

Try eliminating the portion of the cable from the towers to the anchorage (leaving only the portion of the cable from the bridge deck to the towers). *What happens when you test your bridge with a load tester now? Why?*

EXTRA

Try this activity a few more times and focus on what part (or parts) of the bridge fails first. *Was the failure due to weakness of the materials used or weakness at a joint? Can you think of ways to redesign your bridge to make the part (or parts) that failed stronger?*

OBSERVATIONS AND RESULTS

Did the suspension bridge hold a greater number of coins compared with the beam bridge?

In this activity, you should have seen that the suspension bridge was able to hold more coins than the beam bridge by around 150 percent, such as about 310 pennies (or 140 quarters) compared with about 200 pennies (or 90 quarters). When the beam bridge failed, this was likely because the deck straw bent downward as more coins were added, until it bent so much that it slipped down between the two towers. As coins were added to the suspension bridge, the cable (that is, the thread) was under tension and reinforced the bridge deck straw, pulling it upward (while compressing the towers) and allowing the bridge to hold more coins. When the suspension bridge eventually failed, the bridge deck straw likely similarly bent into a V shape, but because it was attached by the thread, the straw couldn't fall and instead the cup may have slipped off of the straw.

CLEANUP

Put away the materials you used.
Throw out or recycle any scraps.

THE SCIENTIFIC METHOD

The scientific method helps scientists—and students—gather facts to prove whether an idea is true. Using this method, scientists come up with ideas and then test those ideas by observing facts and drawing conclusions. You can use the scientific method to develop and test your own ideas!

Question: What do you want to learn? What problem needs to be solved? Be as specific as possible.

Research: Learn more about your topic and refine your question.

Hypothesis: Form an educated guess about what you think will answer your question. This allows you to make a prediction you can test.

Experiment: Create a test to learn if your hypothesis is correct. Limit the number of variables, or elements of the experiment that could change.

Analysis: Record your observations about the progress and results of your experiment. Then analyze your data to understand what it means.

Conclusion: Review all your data. Did the results of the experiment match the prediction? If so, your hypothesis was correct. If not, your hypothesis may need to be changed.

GLOSSARY

adjacent: Next to or near something.
comprise: To be made up of.
corrugated: Having a wavy surface.
diameter: A straight line that runs from one side of a figure and passes through the center.
displacement: The removal of something from its usual place or position by something which then occupies that place or position.
engineering: The application of science to the goal of creating useful machines or structures.
geometry: A branch of mathematics that deals with points, lines, angles, surfaces, and solids.
innovative: Original and creative.
pantograph: A jointed framework.
physics: A science that deals with the facts about matter and motion and includes the subjects of mechanics, heat, light, electricity, sound, and the atomic nucleus.
pivot: A shaft or pin with a pointed end on which something turns, or the action of turning around this point.
ratio: The relationship in number or quantity between two or more things.
rigid: Not flexible.
skewer: A pin of wood or metal, often used for fastening meat to keep it in form while roasting or to hold small pieces of meat or vegetables for broiling.
suspension: The state of being hung from something.
variable: Something that changes or can be changed.

ADDITIONAL RESOURCES

Books

Borgert-Spaniol, Megan. *Engineering You Can Eat.* Minneapolis, MN: Super Sandcastle, 2019.

Herkert Schul, Christina, and Paige Green. *Awesome Engineering Activities for Kids: 50+ Exciting STEAM Projects to Design and Build.* Emeryville, CA: Rockridge Press, 2019.
Websites

Websites

Discovery Education
sciencefaircentral.com

Exploratorium
www.exploratorium.edu/search/science%20fair%20projects

Science Buddies
www.sciencebuddies.org/science-fair-projects/project-ideas/list

Science Fun
www.sciencefun.org/?s=science+fair

Videos

"Biomechanical Engineering"
ny.pbslearningmedia.org/resource/biomechanical-engineering-your-future/biomechanical-engineering-video/, PBS Learning Media, 6:56.

"Photonics Engineering"
ny.pbslearningmedia.org/resource/phototonics-engineering-your-future/engineering-your-future-video/, PBS Learning Media, 11:46.

Publisher's note to educators and parents: Our editors have carefully reviewed these websites to ensure that they are suitable for students. Many websites change frequently, however, and we cannot guarantee that a site's future contents will continue to meet our high standards of quality and educational value. Be advised that students should be closely supervised whenever they access the internet.

INDEX